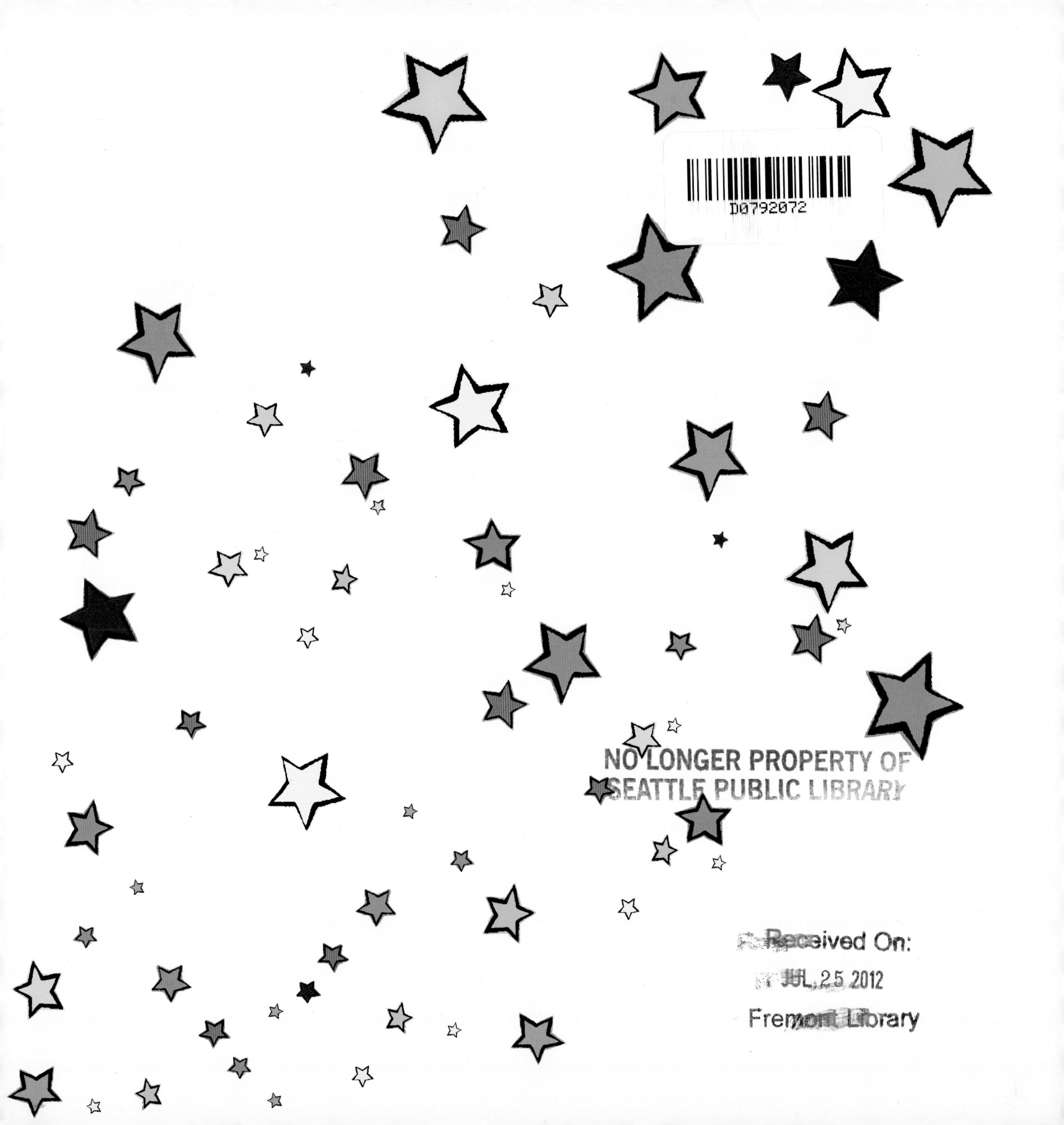

For Eunice and Maria
with love and thanks
—Emma

Foxy

For information address HarperCollins Children's Books, a division of HarperCollins Publishers, 10 East 53rd Street, New York, NY 10022.
www.harpercollinschildrens.com

Library of Congress Cataloging-in-Publication Data
Dodd, Emma, date.
Foxy / Emma Dodd. — 1st ed.
p. cm.
Summary: Emily is worried about starting school for the first time, but Foxy waves his magic tail to provide what she needs to be ready.
ISBN 978-0-06-201419-1 (trade bdg.)
[1. First day of school—Fiction. 2. Magic—Fiction. 3. Foxes—Fiction.] I. Title.
PZ7.R27377Fox 2012 2010045555
[E]—dc22 CIP
AC

Typography by Dana Fritts
12 13 14 15 16 SCP 10 9 8 7 6 5 4 3 2 1 ❖ First Edition

Emma Dodd

Foxy

HARPER
An Imprint of HarperCollins*Publishers*

It was way past bedtime. Tomorrow was Monday, and Emily would be starting school.

Emily sat up in bed. She looked worried.

"What's the matter?" asked Foxy.
"Whatever it is, I'm sure I can help."

"I'm worried I haven't got all the things
I need for the first day of school," said Emily.

Foxy wanted to help Emily, and he thought he would be able to with his magic tail. Foxy waved it back and forth and back and forth so Emily would notice.

"I don't need a tail for school," said Emily. "I need a **pencil**."

"Voilà!

A pencil!" said Foxy.

"No, silly, that's a **penguin!**" said Emily.

Foxy tried again, and this time he came up with a pencil.

"Now I need a **pencil case,**" said Emily.

"Thank you, Foxy. I also have to bring a **notebook.**"

"TA-DA!

A notebook!"

"I guess magic is hard," said Emily.

"Oops, let me try that again."

"That's better!"

"And here's an
eraser. . . ."
UH-OH!

"I'd love some new **school shoes,**" Emily suggested.

"Thank you, Foxy," Emily said politely. "But I think I'll wear my boots to school instead."

"How about a new **hat?"** asked Foxy.

". . . Never mind, I'll wear it myself."

"And here's a **schoolbag!**"

"No, silly, that's a **pirate flag**!"

Emily still looked worried.

"*Now* what's the matter?" asked Foxy.

"What if I am not smart enough?" asked Emily.

Foxy touched Emily with his magic tail.

"Oh dear," said Emily. "I think I would rather learn these things at school."

"And one last thing . . . ," said Emily. "What if nobody likes me?"
"Now, you don't need my magic for that, Emily," said Foxy.

"I know you'll make plenty of friends."

SCHOOL